Enis and Emma

Tail of a Brother and Sister

by

Niki Rolen

AuthorHouse™
1663 Liberty Drive, Suite 200
Bloomington, IN 47403
www.authorhouse.com
Phone: 1-800-839-8640

AuthorHouse™ UK Ltd.
500 Avebury Boulevard
Central Milton Keynes, MK9 2BE
www.authorhouse.co.uk
Phone: 08001974150

This book is a work of fiction. People, places, events, and situations are the product of the author's imagination. Any resemblance to actual persons, living or dead, or historical events, is purely coincidental.

First published by AuthorHouse 6/26/2007

ISBN: 978-1-4259-5782-7 (sc)

Printed in the United States of America
Bloomington, Indiana

This book is printed on acid-free paper.

Bloomington, IN  Milton Keynes, UK

authorHOUSE®

Dedication

This book is dedicated to you, Raine, and all the lives you will touch. During the book's first stage of completion, your mother, the author, is eight months pregnant with you. Your daddy, Scott, and your brother and sister, Enis and Emma, are anxiously awaiting your arrival. –November 2004.

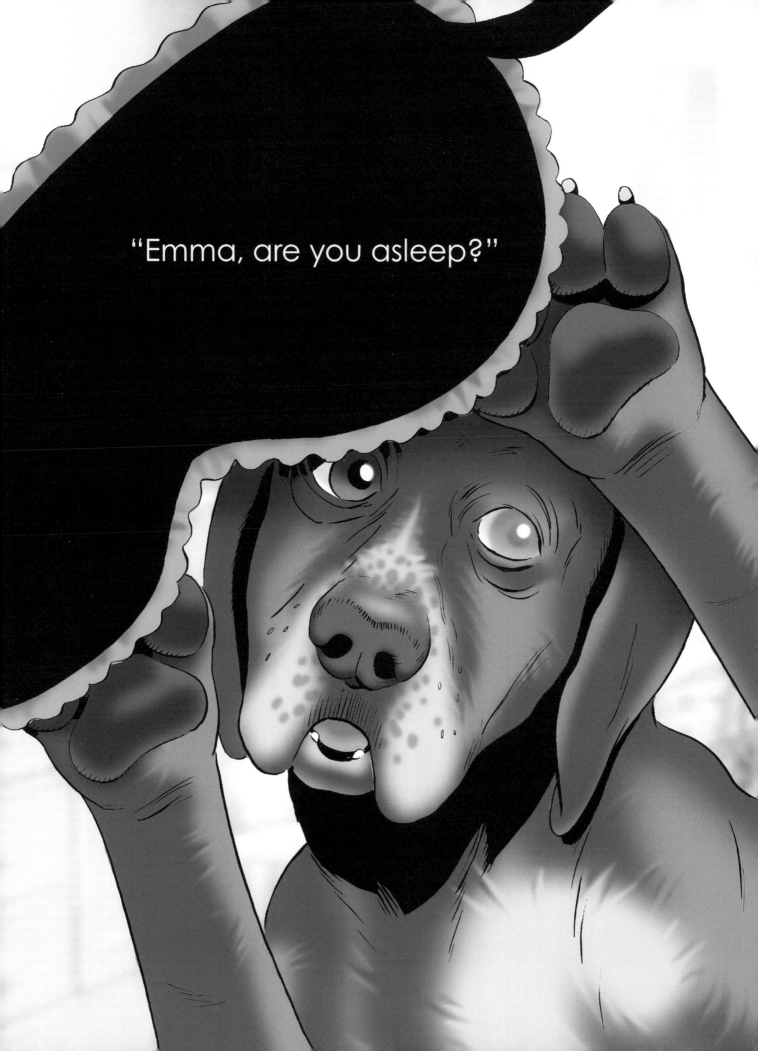

"How can I sleep when your breath stinks and you're standing on my ear?" Emma said with a yawn.

"I had lamb and rice for breakfast!" Enis said a little too loudly. "It was delicious!"

"Did I mention you're standing on my ear?" said the ninety-pound, shiny black Labrador.

"Well spotted, Emma!" Enis shouted. "You should've said something!"

"Good night!" Emma said stretching her long legs.

"I am quite sure it's morning," Enis said, tilting his head.

"It is morning," Emma stated.

"Glorious! Let's go to the park and…PLAY BALL!" Enis howled. "Shine and rise!"

"It's rise and shine," Emma said with a wrinkled brow.

Enis just stared at Emma, blinking slowly with soft eyes. One eye was completely clouded from a cataract. She wondered if he could see out of it at all.

"Before we go to the park, please go brush your teeth," Emma reminded Enis as she slipped her paw under her pillow and gave her lucky rock a rub.

So Enis ran and dipped his Nyla bone in chicken-flavored pooch paste and grabbed his tattered satchel of Wilson #2 tennis balls. Emma put on her pink tutu for the trip.

At the bus stop, Enis stood way too close to Emma, wrinkling her tutu. He pointed his freckled snout to the sky and loudly barked, "WHAT A BEAUTIFUL DAY, EMMA, JUST SPEC-TACULAR!"

Emma wondered if Enis's cataract affected his hearing.

"How does my tutu look?"she asked while dancing around on her tiptoes.

Enis stalled a bit then replied, "You're not exactly a dainty poodle, Emma, but you do have some outstanding circus qualities!"

"Surely you didn't just say circus," Emma asked.

"Who's Shirley?" Enis replied.

Suddenly a gust of dusty wind blew Enis and Emma's ears straight up as the bus skidded to a stop.

"I think I have a scratched cornea!" Enis bellowed while blinking his eyes. Emma sneezed.

As the dust settled, the doors flew open. The driver chimed, "Hey baby what's shakin'? Beautiful day! Where ya headed? Bowling alley, grocery store, library?"

"Hello, Biscuits!" Enis hollered. "We're going to the park to…PLAY BALL!"

Biscuits grinned from ear to ear. "Hey baby, that's great!"

"Didn't you used to work at the hot dog stand, Biscuits?" Emma asked.

"Hey baby, got canned last week, picked up this job a few days later. Somebody has to bring home the bacon for my sister Ruby. She's a squirrel watcher; not a very steady income for us."

"A SQUIRREL WATCHER! THAT SOUNDS ADVENTUROUS!" Enis shouted excitedly.

Biscuits tilted her head to one side. "Hey baby, is there something wrong with your hearing?"

"What?" Enis replied.

A few stops later, the bus was screeching to a halt as Biscuits slammed on the brakes. Emma thought for sure she had whiplash.

"We're here!" Enis jumped up and hit his head on the top of the bus. Tennis balls scattered everywhere. He leapt over Emma, somehow stepping on her with all four paws. Then he ran down the isle, turned the corner, fell down the stairs, and smashed into the bus doors!

"Hey baby, that had to hurt!" Biscuits said as she opened the doors.

Emma barreled to the front, her heart pounding. "Enis, are you all right? You scared the tar out of me!"

"Fourteen hundred ninety two, Columbus sailed the ocean blue!" Enis shouted in a daze.

"Hey baby, don't leave without one of these."
Biscuits pulled a pooper scooper from her very
long vest.

"Good night! Put that thing away!" Emma felt
like everyone was watching. "Who carries their
own you-know-what around?"

"Hey Baby suit yourself. A clean park is a happy park. No scooper, no problem. How about a golf club?"

"I have no thumbs," Emma said, shaking her head.

"Antique china?"

"I'm all thumbs," Emma replied.

"What about breath mints!" Biscuits said with determination. "Cures every form of morning breath!"

Emma's ears perked up. "Now that he needs— I mean we need," Emma quickly corrected herself. She didn't want to hurt her brother's feelings. "Thanks, Biscuits."

"Hey baby, no problem!" Biscuits said, satisfied.

"Emma, why would we need breath mints?" Enis asked, perplexed.

"Fresh breath is always a priority," Emma stated like a beauty pageant contestant.

"I'll have to remember that," Enis said with great seriousness.

They both waved goodbye to Biscuits as she squealed away out of sight, swerving down the street.

Once inside the park, Emma's body stiffened. Her eyes were wide and her ears forward. Enis listened intensely. "What is it, Emma?"

"Geese!" she whispered. "Sounds like hundreds in the lake!"

"Emma, don't you dare! They'll peck your eyes out!"

"I'm a Labrador, Enis," Emma calmly explained. "It's in my breed. Besides, I'm only going to scare them a little, nothing too dramatic." But Emma wasn't telling the entire truth.

"I WILL NOT be held responsible for your actions, Emma!"

It was too late. Emma had made up her mind. "Here Enis," Emma said, her eyes still fixed toward the lake. "Hold my tutu! I'm going in!"

And she took off like the wind! When she reached the edge of the lake she took a bounding leap! Enis could see her in the air, her black coat shining, her long ears flying. Then down she went, heavy, and belly flopped into the lake, producing the most amazing tidal wave. Geese flew up everywhere, covering the sky, honking angry goose words.

"Just sickening," Enis said turning away. "Despicable!"

Emma pulled herself out of the lake, saturated with water. "Did you see that?" she beamed. "That was the best belly flop I've done all year! I should win a medal in the Great Outdoor Games for that one!"

"I doubt they would award a medal to a bully," Enis said, disgusted. "Here's your tutu. I'm going to pick some wildflowers."

"YOU SAID YOU'RE GOING TO TAKE A SHOWER!" Emma hollered, shaking her head. She seemed to have a little water in her ears.

"PICK WILDFLOWERS!" Enis yelled as loudly as he could.

"You're not allowed to pick wildflowers here," Emma reminded him as she stepped into her tutu, still wet.

"Then I'll just be sniffing them," Enis decided.

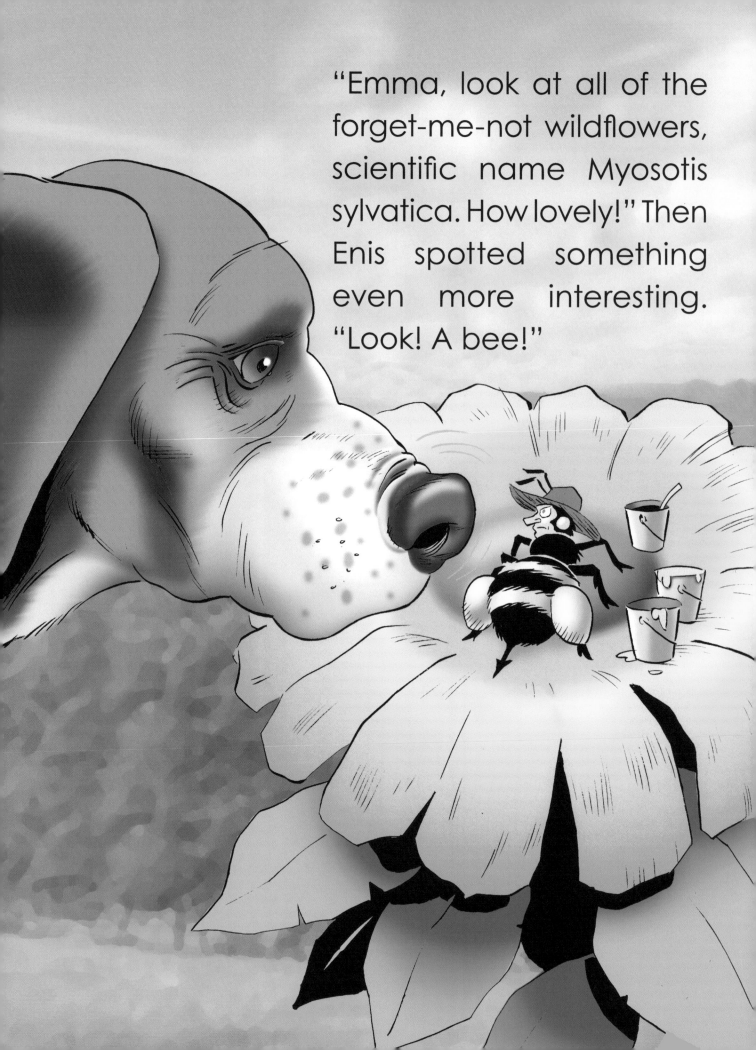

"Emma, look at all of the forget-me-not wildflowers, scientific name Myosotis sylvatica. How lovely!" Then Enis spotted something even more interesting. "Look! A bee!"

"Bees are actually very friendly, Emma. They're not aggressive like many people think they are. Did you know bees pollinate many of the foods we eat? What a wonderful flying insect!"

Emma was shocked at Enis's knowledge of flowers and bees but complete lack of common sense all at the same time. She watched Enis nervously as he followed the bee to every flower.

Emma could see the bee was getting scared and frustrated.

"Enis," Emma stated sternly, "it's best just to respect his space."

"If I could just get a closer look," Enis said, sniffing the bee, "I might discover the secret to pollination."

And before Emma could say another word, Enis shouted, "FORGET-ME-NOT! That was a good one!"

The bee had stung Enis on the nose and buzzed away very upset.

"See!" Emma shouted. "I told you to respect his space!"

"Do you happen to have any calamine lotion on hand?" Enis responded, licking his nose.

"You are completely missing the point!" Emma cried. "It's not your place to be in his space."

"Emma, that rhymes. Ha! You could be a poet!" Enis loudly announced.

"Forget it!" Emma exclaimed. "You're never going to get it!"

"You did it again, Emma! Brilliant!"

"GOOD NIGHT!" Emma shrieked.

"I am quite sure it's about midday," Enis said, looking up at the sun. "But they do say canines have no sense of real time."

Emma looked weak. "I'm going to find a shady spot under the weeping willow," she whimpered. "Wake me up in an hour or so."

"Will do, my little ballerina!" Enis chimed.

Emma walked away slowly, her head low, her eyes heavy. Enis would be okay by himself for a while.

As Enis watched Emma disappear, he suddenly realized what he had come for. "PLAY BALL!" he shouted like an umpire. Enis looked down at his satchel. His tail wagged wildly. He plunged his entire head into the bag and madly sniffed every corner of it. Soon Enis's tail slowed down and eventually…sank to the ground. There were huge frayed holes in the bottom of the bag. All of his Wilson #2's were gone. He had been dragging it around completely empty and didn't even notice.

Like a regal prince, Enis sat down and waited. As a soft breeze passed by, he pointed his white freckled nose upward toward the warm sun. There seemed to be something very tiny suspended above him, swaying in the light wind. He wasn't quite sure what it was, and in a moment, she came into focus.

"Ello, Enis," the spider said, lowering down to Enis's snout.

"Hello," Enis replied, tilting his head. "How do you know my name?"

"Oh I know everyone who comes to this park," she claimed confidently. "It's quite lovely. That's why I've decided to build my flat here."

"What's a flat?" Enis asked.

"A flat is where I live. That's what we call it in England."

"England!" Enis said surprised. "How did you get here?"

"Oh it was quite easy really. I came over on holiday—on the Queen Mary II cruise ship.

Smashing rates for a species like me. I've been all over this brilliant country."

"Then you know what a Wilson #2 tennis ball looks like," Enis said joyfully.

"I think I do," said the spider as she rocked back and forth with the wind. Enis was so close to her he could see himself in her glassy eyes. She didn't seem to mind.

"Do you know where I could find one?" Enis asked.

"I know of many lost items in the park. There was a ball left here ages ago but, pity, I believe it was a Wilson #3," the spider recalled.

"Anything will do!" Enis said desperately. "A Wilson #2, Wilson #3, even a Penn model. Please tell me where it is!"

"I'm afraid it's a bit dodgy, Enis. It's at the bottom of the lake. Might you know of any expert swimmers?" she suggested.

"I know the greatest swimmer in the world!" Enis said proudly.

"Hurry along and fetch her," the spider said anxiously. "No need to lag about."

"Thank you, Mrs...Excuse me, what was your name?" Enis had forgotten to ask. He lowered his head and felt embarrassed at his lack of manners.

"Hang on to your chin strap, Enis! My name is Lady Eleanor." Enis raised his head. His eyes were sparkling.

"Thank you, Lady Eleanor. I'll never forget you."

"Nor will I you," she responded. And off Enis went to find the greatest swimmer he had ever known. "Such a gentle-hearted lad," Lady Eleanor stated aloud as Enis disappeared in the low sun. "He has the eyes of a wise old soul."

Enis was racing! Lady Eleanor's voice was in his head, inspiring him. He soon caught a scent of lake water and down feathers. It was Emma! He quickened his pace. At the top of a hill the great weeping willow stood. There he found Emma, her paws twitching wildly in her deep sleep.

"EMMA!" Enis screeched.

Emma gave a loud snort and jumped to her feet. "INTRUDER!" she howled. "SECURITY BREECH!"

"Where?" Enis shouted as he jerked his head side to side.

"Sorry," Emma said in a low voice. "I was dreaming."

Enis wasted no time. "Emma, I've acquired the exact location of a Wilson #3!"

"A what?" Emma's brow wrinkled with question.

"A Wilson #3!" Enis went on. "Queen Eleanor of England has come over on a flat lady ship for the holidays with information of a Wilson #3! It's at the bottom of Lake Dodge! There's to be no lagging about!" And with that said, Enis sprinted off straight for the lake.

"What?" Emma said to herself. "Queen Eleanor, Lake Dodge?"

Emma caught up with Enis at the lake's edge. A part-pointer and part-retriever, Enis pointed his nose to the lake and raised one paw off the ground. Emma knew not to question Enis. She stepped in the direction of his snout and swam silently to the middle of the lake. Slight ripples in the water followed behind her.

She took a deep breath and plunged her head and shoulders downward. She twisted her body like a corkscrew and fiercely kicked her back legs. Her paws opened up like great fans as she pushed against the water. From the surface, there was a great splash, then silence. Enis waited, his body motionless. In a tree nearby, Lady Eleanor was watching. She had great hope for Emma.

Just below the water's surface, there were thousands of tiny fish in a rainbow of florescent colors. Their bodies reflected the light of the low evening sun as if they were wearing sequins. Emma noticed the water becoming colder and the light from the surface was fading. She opened her eyes wide to see a school of much bigger fish hovering above a slimy wall of seaweed. They were hiding from the fisherman and darted out of the way as Emma approached. As the seaweed clung to her thick coat of fur, she broke through the wall like a big black bear. It was there Enis's ball appeared! She started toward it when something else caught her attention.

There seemed to be a glistening in the distance. Emma headed toward the brightness. The closer she got, the more it glowed! Finally she was upon it! It was like gold to her hidden at the bottom of the lake, with no one to behold it! She was beginning to lose most of her breath as a few bubbles escaped from her nose. She opened her mouth and freed it from the mud. Its surface glistened. It was the most beautiful rock she had ever seen.

As Emma swam away, she looked back at the beaten-up, muddy tennis ball. She knew that ball was gold to Enis. It reminded her of how much he believed in her. Without another thought, she let the rock go as it sparkled its way to the dark floor. She gave a few good thrusts toward the ball and with one swift movement was on her way to the surface, the Wilson #3 in her possession!

She broke the surface with a loud spray of air from her nose. Enis danced in circles and shouted, "YOU DID IT, EMMA! I KNEW YOU COULD DO IT!"

Emma felt wonderful! Enis was wild with happiness! She pulled herself out of the water and gave a great shake. "Emma, you gave me quite a scare!" Enis said nervously. "I was going to come in after you!"

"I started getting nervous myself," Emma admitted. "There are some weird fish down there!"

"All creatures are vital to the eco system, Emma," Enis said knowingly.

"Let's go home, Enis" Emma was pooped.

As they started to make their way home together, Lady Eleanor smiled as she watched them leave.

"Brilliant species," she whispered. "Love to you, my darlings."

As they reached the outside of the park, Enis asked, "How can I ever thank you, Emma?"

"Let me sleep in tomorrow," Emma said, smiling as she handed Enis a mint for his breath.

"Oh Emma, you're quite a card," Enis joked as he swallowed the mint whole.

At that moment a light rain began to fall. Enis pointed his freckles to the sky and gave a few sniffs. "Smells like rain," he said with a smile. "Oh how I love rain, don't you, Emma?"

"I do," Emma replied, looking up, batting her eyes in the light mist. "I really do."

Printed in the United States
87167LV00001BA